The Foundlings
and the
Fisherman
from Tumby

Phillip Leighton-Daly

Ordering Information:

Prime Seven Media
518 Landmann St.
Tomah City, WI 54660

Printed in the United States of America

Books by the Author

Non-fiction

* <u>Recollections of the Central Coast NSW</u> – 2004 – Goulburn. ISBN 646-444252.

* Reflective History of the Goulburn District Volume I. – <u>Life's Hard School</u> – 2010. Goulburn. ISBN 9780980809305.

* Reflective History of the Goulburn District Volume II. – <u>Taking a Chance</u> – 2010. Goulburn. ISBN 97809809312.

* A Reflective History of the Goulburn District Volume III.– <u>But of the Hut I Built</u>. – 2010. Goulburn. ISBN 9780980809329.

* A Reflective History of the Goulburn District Volume IV – <u>The Tides and the Lives of Men.</u> 2016. Goulburn. ISBN 9780980809343.
   This book won the 2015 Goulburn – Mulwaree Heritage Award for historical research. "Preserving Goulburn – Mulwaree's Heritage."

* A Reflective History of the Goulburn District Volume V – <u>Wrinkled Armpits and Woollybutts</u> – The Past and Present Significance of Native Flora in the Goulburn District, 2017. Goulburn. ISBN 9780980809350.

* Kenmore Psychiatric Hospital. <u>Wednesday's Child</u>. – Goulburn. This book won the 2014 Goulburn – Mulwaree Heritage Award for historical research.

* Recollections of Wider Goulburn – <u>Hither, Thither and Yon</u>. 2018, 9780980809367.

* Reflections of the Goulburn District. <u>The Towrang Stockade</u>. Goulburn. 2018. 9780980808381.

* <u>Mouldering Treasures of a Psychiatric Hospital, Volume I</u>, <u>A Photographic Compilation of Kenmore</u>, 2020, 9780980809374.

* <u>Mouldering Treasures of a Psychiatric Hospital, Volume II</u>, <u>Kenmore</u>, 9780980809398.

* <u>Mouldering Treasures of a Psychiatric Hospital, Kenmore</u>, Volume III, 97806451718.

* <u>Goulburn's Orphanage of St John</u>, <u>Inspirational Christian Charity Over 65 Years</u>, 9780648608608.

Young Adult Fiction

The Prince who Wanted to Live Forever.

The Fisherman and his Foundlings.

Elizabeth's Garden.

The Crinkling on the Pie.

No Honor Among Thieves.

The Boiling Toad.

The Feral Menace.

Honorable Thieves.

Rowing against the Tide.

The Crinkling on the Poisonous Pie.

Contents

William Quantrill

In 1863, Confederate Captain William Quantrill and his 400 horsemen torched our Kansas town of Lawrence. During this tirade of insanity, over 160 men, women and children were butchered; over 180 buildings were destroyed.

Prior to the massacre, random spot fires had flared between our Jayhawkers and Quantrill's men. The conflagration at Lawrence was fueled by the imprisonment and deaths of female pro slavery sympathizers.

The horrific murder of the men, women and children was devastating for us, the anti-slave supporters. Few residents were as tragically affected as our family. My name is Jon Treves and my wife is Margaret. By the day's end, the forlorn bodies of our eight-year-old twins, Joseph and Jacob lay amongst the slain. There appeared no limit to Quantrill's savagery. Civilians and children were all targeted, even eight-year-olds deemed capable of bearing arms.

Though Quantrill received a commission for his cowardly massacres of anti-slavery sympathizers, events did not always run to plan. Rallying at Lawrence, Jayhawkers and several abolitionists, myself included, reined heavy fire upon Quantrill's men. I have always paraded as an ardent abolitionist - an anti-slave sympathizer. My deadly beads on the raiders at Lawrence bought several to the ground.

Outraged by the loss of his veterans, and before leaving the field, Quantrill levelled this blood-chilling admonishment at us. "Cowardly curs beware, over the next month, I shall hunt you and your families down; I shall send you all to hell."

Within that month, as Quantrill had promised, he and his raiders returned and ambushed a dozen anti-slave sympathizers. But alas, on close inspection of the dead, Margaret and my bodies were absent. Quantrill's devious reprisal had failed. My wife and I had departed for Australia the previous week.

The Lurcher

Charles Webster was the first mate on the Morning Mist. A whisker short of six feet, he was very strong and fit. Charles reportedly was the first to trim the sails in a squall, to deploy the lifeboats and to navigate through difficult waters.

Charles was a formidable seaman and well respected by most who had the pleasure to meet him.

One day prior to boarding the Morning Mist, my wife and I met Charles, a man who would play an integral part in our lives. We found him perched on the edge of a long wharf, his legs dangling downward towards the water. He had an obvious fascination with tall ships; he sat peering out to sea. A large hunting hound called Marley lay alongside him, her head lovingly resting on his thigh.

Such a trusting friendship was hard to understand. Dog and owner had scarcely known one another for one week. Charles explained the curious events to us.

"Marley was a famed champion in the district. People called her The Lurcher. Crowds amassed to watch her hunt. Her achievements were legendary.

"As Marley aged, her performances diminished and she was grievously mistreated. One afternoon I felt obliged to intervene. Through no fault of her own, Marley was being mercilessly lashed. Tearing the whip from the beast's hand, I turned it upon him. Then picking up the distressed animal, I carried him to the police station. Marley's weak and emaciated condition aroused immediate concern amongst the officers.

"During her halcyon years, Marley had chased red and grey foxes, coyotes, bob cats, rabbits and hares. Being able to reach speeds of up to 40 mph, few can match her for speed and agility. She had been mauled by a coyote. Grey foxes had eluded her by climbing trees or scrambling into dense prickly thickets. Jackrabbits had outpaced her with zig zagging and leaping counter measures. From experience Marley had learned not to engage mountain lions. They were faster and outweighed her by as much as one hundred and forty pounds.

"Marley was special for another reason. Many hunting champions possessed acute senses of smell. Marley's hearing and sight were well advanced and decidedly superior to our own.

"Marley lay on the floor of the police station as a broken - down plug, a mere shadow of her former self. Several ribs had been broken and her upper jaw had been so badly beaten that over time it had shriveled. Her teeth permanently protruded from under it.

"The Hound Hunting Association deeply resented the treatment that their president received. Apparently, it was adjudged permissible to cruelly mistreat one's dogs similarly to colored slaves! The Association openly proclaimed that presidents George Washington and Thomas Jefferson owned hunting dogs. This was license enough to operate outside the law. Interference from all, including the police, was deeply resented. With strong support from the president's rank and file, two thugs were employed to 'bring Marley and me to heel'.

"An assault was organized late at night. I live in a ketch moored to a 200- foot wharf. Suspecting some reprisal from the Hunting Association, a policeman was charged with patrolling that precinct prior to my departure on the Morning Mist.

"It was while the policeman was furthest from the wharf that the thugs appeared as menacing shadows. As I dozed on my bunk, Marley lay curled beside me, her hearing deftly attuned for intruders.

"Then perceiving a sound she watched their approach. Springing at the foremost thug as a rampaging wolf, her impetus sent him toppling into an irresistible ebb current. Aroused by the commotion, I easily accosted the other.

"Several hundred yards out to sea, a half-drowned water rat was manhandled into a rowboat. Hardly in a state to resist and unwilling to solely burden the blame, both quickly revealed the association's involvement. All were adjudged guilty of criminal intent.

"Furthermore, while I was overseas, the police included the wharf district into their daily jurisdiction. The Hunting Association would feel inclined to seek retribution. To find my home drowned at her moorings was a nightmare I dared not entertain!"

Buffeted by the Great Westerlies

"My decision to accept the position of first mate on the Morning Mist was a difficult one. Where did Marley fit into this? She was my responsibility now; she was totally dependent on me. She couldn't be left in San Francisco with the devious members of the hunting fraternity on the loose.

"But conversely, neither were the Morning Mist or her captain held in high regard. Scurrilous innuendoes circulated around the harbors about them. And where dogs were welcome distractions for passengers and crew on long voyages, not so on this ship. No animals of any type were permitted on this vessel.

"With no other vessels seeking a first mate, and the relentless call of the sea a constant torment for me, I felt drawn to sign up on the Morning Mist. But no, the captain was adamant that Marley would not embark.

"As the ship's departure-time loomed, and with no first mate, the captain's resolve weakened. Marley and I found ourselves aboard the three-masted schooner bound for Australia. But was it the right decision? Early indicators were that it wasn't!"

Most of the crew and passengers warmed to Marley immediately. When Charles was aloft trimming the sails or at the helm, the dog circulated around the deck muzzling the passengers affectionately. When Marley placed her paw on the passenger's knee, she most often received tasty morsels as a reward. But when Charles returned from his duties, Marley had only time for him.

In the main, the captain was perpetually inebriated and in that belligerent state, he pretended that Marley didn't exist. Two days into the voyage, Marley strayed in front of him. In a fit of anger, he kicked her savagely. "Get out of my way you weevilly bag of bones."

Charles was instantly upon him. With little respect for authority, he roared, "Do that again and the Morning Mist will need another captain." And this formidable man stared daggers at the captain as a fox does a chicken.

Steerage

Distraught and impoverished after the loss of our children and our home, we barely funded our voyage across the Pacific. Uncomfortably accommodated in the bowels of the ship, the journey appeared to take an eternity. Lighting, heating and ventilation were all poor. With the danger of fire ever present and near impossible to contain, severe restrictions were placed on lanterns or candles. The wooden vessel was a tinderbox, containing straw mattresses, hemp ropes, and tar calking.

Steerage passengers were treated as piranhas in 19th century sailing vessels. Wealth, education and social status were determining factors. In the minds of some higher paying emigrants, steerage was the pits; its passengers were deemed miserable and undeserving.

Poorly provisioned, we lived as paupers. Whereas the wealthy passengers brought biscuits, cheese, ham and eggs on board, we had no such luxuries. And whereas the wealthy were well outfitted with changeable clothing, Margaret and I were poorly provisioned. Most male passengers had three flannel shirts, six pairs of stockings and six long pants at their disposal. The women had six pairs of stockings, four petticoats, a cloak and dresses in large trunks. We possessed two changes of clothing which were hardly adequate for the variable oceanic conditions.

The ship's regulations reeked of class distinction too. Steerage personnel were not permitted to visit other passengers, unless invited. We were excluded from dances, musical performances, saloons and other social activities.

Steerage passengers had no cabins. We spent our passage confined in cargo bays, the males in the bow, married couples amidships, and the single females at the stern. Single female quarters were off limits to the males. A portly matron called Martha, strictly enforced a 9 pm curfew.

Margaret cooked my meals. Rice pudding, sea pie, pea soup and oatmeal porridge were common features on our menu.

Though the passage appeared a slow arduous drudgery for us, not so the captain. He saw it most favorable. Buffeted by the Great Westerlies, features of the Australian coastline loomed before us after two months. This was half the average crossing time, comparable with the passages of steam driven vessels.

Such large voyages were in their development stage in the 1860s, their reliability over long distances yet established. The availability of vital infrastructure and resources such as coal were other determining factors.

One highlight of our crossing was a friendship struck with two first class passengers. A German couple, Ida and Isador Strausen established an amiable relationship with us. We enjoyed sumptuous afternoon teas in their cabin complete with ham, cheeses, and biscuits. The kindly couple supplied us with additional clothing too. And fine, expensive clothes they were. Isador was the manager of a large department store in Manhattan.

There was much to talk about, our wives discussed women's dress fashions in Manhattan. Isador and I were interested in the development of the American Transcontinental Railway. The Chinese contribution was of key interest to us.

We enjoyed our brief time together immensely and vowed that we would actively pursue our friendship. Intervening events would make that impossible!

The Pretenders

First and second-class paying passengers aboard the Morning Mist generally saw themselves superior to those in steerage. They avoided us where ever possible. And this was a safe course of action in regard to two weird passengers. The married couple insisted they were celebrated actors and musicians. The female claimed she was the daughter of an acclaimed actor called John Wilkes Booth, the man who assassinated President Lincoln. The man paraded around in a Confederate officer's uniform. He boasted that he had apprehended freedom fighter, John Brown at Harpers Ferry in 1859, that he was instrumental too in his sentencing and a witness at the hanging. He claimed he was an English aristocrat, a recent immigrant, one of a family of twelve. To be frank, he claimed a lot of things and we didn't believe them!

Both were loud, obnoxious steerage passengers who drank heavily and argued continuously. To the disgust and annoyance of most on board, they frequently played rousing inflammatory songs, songs like the Southern Soldier. Not all on board warmed to these lyrics. *"I place my knapsack on my back, my rifle on my shoulder. I march away to the firing line and kill a Yankee Soldier."* [1]

Complaints by most on board forced the captain reluctantly to limit singing and musical accompaniment to one hour every day on the poop deck. Despite this, these reprobates succeeded in making themselves

---

[1] Public Domain. Portion of the Confederate Song titled Southern Soldier written circa 1860.

unpopular with most people aboard. Imagine being isolated in a small ship's cargo bay for two months with them?

Regardless of their moods, whether fair or foul, they referred affectionately to each other as Del and Cass. These were the couple's affectionate, odd-ball titles for Delila and Cassanova. This was particularly annoying for many on board. During their belligerent arguments, this amiability persisted. And when one asked a question of the other, they responded with a nursery rhyme. When absent for a period, Delila would ask, "Dearest Cassanova where have you been?"

And he would respond, "I've been to London to visit the Queen!"

In royal garb, complete with crown and sceptre they often paraded throughout the ship insisting passengers bow down, pay homage and tithing. And although the steerage passengers were supposedly confined to the bowels of the ship, the captain's leniency allowed them to wander around at will!

Much to the constant annoyance of Charles, the pair camped upon the poop deck, a designation off limits to steerage passengers. Though regularly hounded back to steerage, their appalling disobedience persisted. Their whole existence was a mystery! Who supplied them with alcohol? And why did the captain tolerate their mad-cap antics? In his assessment of the captain's leniency towards them, Charles was often seen shaking his head and muttering, 'a cowl does not make a monk.'

Young Pip

Another acquaintance who Margaret and I grew fondly of, was the cabin boy Pip. Raised originally as an orphan, Pip escaped to the dockyards when ten years old. There he found work on the tall ships. An assignment on the Morning Mist was a wonderful opportunity for free meals, lodging and passage around the world.

Young Pip's exuberance and his boyish personality, reminded Margaret and me of our children. Their spirit was closely akin to Pip. For a twelve-year-old he had a keen interest in the American history, in particular, the jayhawkers and Jim Lane, and for the southerners, Quantrill. For one so young, he was particularly knowledgeable. He asked whether I had fired upon members of the James/Younger brothers at Lawrence. They rode with Quantrill in the early years of their lives. When I answered that I was unsure, he added politely, "Mr Treves, I believe Frank and Jesse James joined Quantrill after Lawrence. Cole Younger could have been involved though, for he joined Quantrill in 1862 after the union forces murdered his dad."

"You are well informed young Pip. I would never have recognized Cole Younger anyway; it was very early in his career."

"And Mr Treves, much of the town had been torched; the area would have been blanketed in smoke."

"Indeed it was, my young gentleman."

Being from Kansas, where slave and anti-slave sentiments persisted, both Pip and myself believed massacres of Quantrill and his Union adversary Jim Lane, barbaric. In regard to who was the more grievous, I strongly opted for Quantrill.

"And if I lost my two sons," Pip added, "I would agree with you."

The captain was cruel to Pip. Never once did he offer him one skerrick of encouragement. The captain's caustic criticism of Pip noticeably affected his confidence. I spoke to Pip about this. "When the captain speaks disrespectfully to you, you don't lose respect for him; you lose respect for yourself! Pip, even though you have many supporters on board this ship, you must treat the captain and his buffoons with the upmost care."

And on a more humorous note, I said to him, "Remember when you sup with the devil, use a long spoon." Pip appreciated my candor and my support.

The Fancy Dress Parade

Two weeks into our passage the captain invited most of the ship's compliment to a fancy-dress parade. Even the crew were afforded the opportunity. The duties of the helmsman and lookouts were rotated during this grand event so they could all attend.

So deeply ingrained were the captain's prejudices, no invitations were extended to steerage passengers. But strangely, one full week before the concert, both odd-balls practised for the occasion on the poop deck! Cassanova played the violin; Delila the piccolo.

On the day of the performance, much to the captain's displeasure, all steerage passengers attended! The Strausens had invited them. This was in accord with the rules. First class passengers could invite whoever they liked on social occasions. "To not do so on such a long passage was to incite disharmony and rebellion," Mr Strausen added.

When Isador officially invited the misfits, he was told belligerently, "That will not be necessary," sneered Delila, "We are the belles of the ball."

"We are the hub around which the wheel turns!" Cass sniped with self- indignation.

Whatever this gibberish meant, we weren't entirely sure. It suggested that both were pivotal to the running of the parade or perhaps even the ship!

At the start of the concert, the captain arrived as a heavily intoxicated sulk. He obviously objected to the attendance of the lowly steerage passengers. He made no welcoming address; he delegated that to the two pretenders, Cassanova and Delila!

Cass appeared as the Devil, complete with a tail and horns; Del appeared as Faustus, a wealthy businessman. To signify selling his soul to the devil, Delila removed a smiling, welcoming mask. Cass promptly seized this and placed it in a velvet collection bag. A hideous mask appeared underneath. It was the horrible haggard face of Death. Then roughly seizing her hand, Cass the satanic villain, led the miserable countenance of Delila into the underworld. In this instance it was down the companionway into the bowels of the ship.

Could there ever have been a more disturbing or macabre opening? Silence reigned momentarily, though few, hoping to establish a respectful tone responded politely with a warming applause.

The welcome resulted in an immediate re-emergence of the irreverent pair. Far worse was to follow! Their next item assumed an extreme, political stance, a position which would ultimately lead to prolonged, pointless carnage. Cass sang and Del accompanied him on the piccolo.

"With the Grand Exulted Wizard, we'll stand boldly to fight,
to reign terror on the land, to burn crosses at night.
With hoods on our heads, wIth bibles in our hands,
with the authority of God, we'll assuredly stand." [2]

The poem spoke of the emergence of the Ku Klux Klan, a terrifying canker settling upon the American states in the later part of the 19th century. It had distressing effect on Margaret and me for we had lost

___

2 Battle Hymn of the South, 1861. Public Domain.

two sons in the conflict. Few apart from Pip and the Strausens knew of our tragedy.

Undaunted by the inappropriateness of the material, Faustus and the Devil, still in their costumes, launched into the next item. It was a the folk song called 'Barbara Allen'. Delila's hideously daunting death mask glared down at the audience as she played. A young student, George from steerage led us through the song. But at the end of the performance, and even after the generous applause, George remained distraught. For what appeared an eternity he stood with his head bowed and his hand covering his eyes. 'Barbara Allen' had opened a festering wound. Unexpectedly, Bess, a pretty young lass from steerage, sensed his turmoil; she walked over and wrapped a comforting arm around his shoulder. In that manner, she led him back to his seat. Martha, the matron who was charged with the welfare of the girls, materialized immediately. In the event of inappropriate behavior, she sat down beside them.

Then it was Charles the first mate's turn. He sang a song about Old Balloo. It spoke of a dog's life and death and how he dug a grave with a silver spade. His closing lines ended thus:

> "Old Balloo, you good dog you. I'm a-coming after you."

Most of the audience warmed to Charles's performance. The captain didn't. He and those insensitive pretenders fell irreverently upon their knees. The misfits played mournful notes on their instruments. A handkerchief was produced by the captain who pretended to sob. Then raising his hand beseechingly he said, "Oh please Charles stop it, you're breaking my heart!"

Plainly the captain was drunk. And the two misfits bore resentment towards Charles for his rough-treatment when mustering them back to steerage. The audience, initially shocked, applauded. Sensing a conflagration between Charles and the irreverent three, I moved over to Charles and shook his hand, "Let it go." I said, "You have many supporters here."

But the captain had not finished. Feeling brash in his intoxication, he proceeded to further big-note himself. "Keep that bag of bones out of my sight, Charlie – boy. Sharks like dog-meat."

Silence prevailed. Few would have had spoken so disrespectfully to Charles before and escaped without a beating. But Charles harkened to my advice. Now was not the time or place. Charles would bide his time. Certainly, there would be another opportunity.

But even in this instance, Charles glared threateningly at the captain, his formidable stature striking a resonant chord even in the captain's drunken state. And if only for a brief moment, the captain knew he had overstepped the mark.

Mr Strausen then recited Lewis Carrol's memorable poem The Walrus and the Carpenter. The item spoke much about ingratitude, disrespect, and insincerity. Basically, it could have been titled the Captain and the Odd Couple, but they were too drunk or insensitive to realize that it was a reflection of their shallowness. The Walrus and the Carpenter described how two devious fiends invited a dozen plump oysters for a long walk along the beach. Without remorse they ate them between bread and butter.

My item had much to do about the futility of war. The poem was called 'The Charge of the Light Brigade'. These salient words exemplified my belief that wars achieved little apart from destruction and horrible carnage.

"Cannon to right of them; Cannon to left of them,
Cannon behind them volleyed and thundered;
Stormed at with shot and shell, while horse and hero fell.
They that had fought so well, came through the jaws of Death,
Back from the mouth of Hell, all that was left of them,
Left of the six hundred." [3]

The evening was rounded off with the singing of the folk tune 'Bound for South Australia'. The performances revealed the deep insights into several of the characters, particularly the captain and the two buffoons.

------

[3] Public Domain. The Charge of the Light Brigade by Lord Tennyson. 1854.

A Terrible Deed

One particular morning, Cassanova was found heavily inebriated and alone on the poop deck. "Where is Delila?" he was quizzed on numerous occasions. Seemingly drunk and bewildered he replied, "Am I my wife's keeper?" When further pressed to where she'd been, he replied, "She's gone to London to visit the queen!"

Extensive searches produced nothing. And neither the crew or passengers had any answer. Certainly, they heard a terrible altercation earlier in the night. But Delila had disappeared in the early hours of the morning when most were asleep.

There appeared no answer to the mystery. I felt that Cass was grievously involved, that the nursery rhyme nonsense was a guise, a means of avoiding scrutiny.

But as events unraveled, there was a witness, young Pip. He had witnessed the whole episode. He was alone at the helm while providing brief relief for the captain.

Pip divulged the whole grubby details in confidence to both Isador and me. "Cassanova and Delila had the darkest argument over Delila's inheritance. Both had been drinking heavily in the captain's cabin. After dark the two sat huddled together on a bench on the poop deck. The pair were colorfully attired in weird harlequin costumes reminiscent of a circus parade. Delila was so drunk; she could not maintain an upright position on the bench. Strangely the captain had allowed them to remain there. He made no attempt to usher then back to steerage.

"At an opportune time, when Cassanova believed that the captain was alone at the helm, he draped a heavily rusted anchor chain around

Delila. "How beautiful your crown jewels?" And he fitted a hideous death mask over her head. "Your crown jewels are only surpassed by your natural beauty." He kissed the hideous mask on the lips.

"With little more than a grunt and a moan, Cassanova slung Delila over the side, saying "Forgive me Delila, I just couldn't take anymore."

When the captain returned to the helm, Delila had nestled in the mud one mile or so beneath the surface. Though the deck of the ship was swathed in a cloak of fog, the captain must have suspected that Pip had witnessed the entire incident. Mr Strausen and I agreed to keep this deathly silent. Pip's safety was paramount here.

Pip believed that the captain and Cassanova were complicit. He had witnessed their frivolities in the captain's cabin. Cassanova stored several Beaumont-Adams revolvers there. Nineteen thousand of these formidable weapons had been purchased by the United States' government prior to the Civil War. Both the Union and Confederate forces had them. They were preferred at the time to Samuel Colt's revolvers. Cass owned a light artillery sabre too which held pride of position on the captain's table. It had been requisitioned to both the Union and Confederate officers.

Delila owned a derringer and a pepper pot, the latter being a revolver which sprayed buckshot.

When Pip visited the captain's cabin Delila appeared as 'A queen in her counting house, counting all her money.' Apparently, a fortune in silver and golden coins lay before her.

Death Wish

Sow the Wind and Reap a Whirlwind

The captain of the Morning Mist was a tall, thin and wizened man with 30 years' experience at sea. His hair was black; his lined, leathery skin was a consequence of liquor, tobacco, and exposure to the elements.

After the disappearance of Delila the captain exposed Pip to heightened degrees of danger. The 12-year-old was the first dispatched onto the rigging in the foulest of weather. And during the fiercest of gales, Pip was stationed alone at the helm. Charles was ever watchful lest he be swept overboard. He did his upmost to protect Pip throughout these perilous duties much to the captain's displeasure.

The captain's tolerance towards the pretenders was readily apparent. Never once did he discipline the pair. Charles was always charged with dealing with them. A festering animosity grew between them.

The captain's animosity towards Pip was noted by others too. Isador Strausen mentioned it to me on several occasions. In this instance the captain was a puppeteer and Pip was the puppet. The likeable lad loved his job; he found his duties favorable. Never would he contemplate a return to the orphanage. Nor could he survive on the wharves. Murderous crimes and robberies were common place there.

I took it upon myself to investigate the puzzling events of Delila's disappearance. "Did the captain store chains on the poop deck?"

Charles was adamant that he didn't. "But on the day prior to the Delila's disappearance, the captain ordered me to leave a heavy rusted anchor chain there. Chains are never stored on the poop deck."

"There's no chain there now!" I added.

"That's a mystery," Charles added. "Perhaps it was lost in the storm."

"Quite probably the case," I replied.

For Pip's sake, I even kept this secret from Charles. Whether he associated Delila's disappearance with the chain he did not say. Such a murderous measure was not something one would readily contemplate.

The Shipwreck

As the Morning Mist closed upon the eastern coast of Australia, she was caught in a ferocious storm. "Baton down the hatches," the captain bellowed. All passengers were immediately confined to their quarters, the first and second class to their cabins, and the steerage passengers to their respective cargo bays. In the gloominess of our confinement, we grappled with our fears, sea sickness and the lurching of the ship.

Whatever terror or sickness passengers experienced below decks, were trivial to the seaman upon it. Avoiding the monstrous waves while safely navigating or securing the rigging was fraught with danger.

At 8 pm, during the storm's tempest, a blood-curdling scream resounded on deck, "My God it's another ship. Hard to port!" But the call came too late. The Morning Mist buried her bow deep into the side of the Esperalda, a coastal barque. It was a fatal wound to be sure, much like when a bull drives its horn into the belly of a large adversary.

Instantly the surge of the waves and buoyancy of the two combatants saw the Morning Mist recoil as if to continue to parry, but the Esperalda lay mortally wounded with a grievous wound in her side. Into this, tons of water surged. But regardless of her plight, while still lying indecorous on her side, she struggled to retain her stately personage. And for one minute prior to sinking, she did, much like a queen before her execution. Then as if reconciling herself to a watery fate, she slipped beneath the waves.

Moments prior to her disappearance, a small number of crew materialized on the freighter's deck. But once again, the ocean reasserted itself. The crew were quickly enveloped by a large wave and consumed amidst its tempestuous fury. I presumed them all lost.

The Experalda lay upright on the ocean bed,
a gaping hole in her hull.

The Morning Mist did not escape unhindered. The male steerage passenger compartments quickly flooded and the bow dropped deeper into the water. And as we lost more and more buoyancy, the waves crashed over us. Many of us sheltered on the main deck, thoroughly drenched in our life jackets.

At that point there was a terrible crash and the boat shuddered. The lurching had stopped and we found ourselves lodged on a reef. Though this provided temporary relief, it did little to allay our fears. The waves pummeled us incessantly and the treacherous currents swirled hungrily about. Would we soon join the Esperalda on the bottom?

It was not until the early hours of the morning did those fierce winds abate. But what a surprise! As daylight dawned, the mainland loomed tantalizingly close. Several distinctive features were apparent. A towering rocky bluff resembled a powerful defiant hand. A huge rocky arch spanned a channel of water. Behind, the escarpment ran to the north and south as far as the eye could see.

"It is proposed to launch the lifeboats in the afternoon," said the captain, a man of few words. "The seas will be calmer and we'll reach the mainland in the lifeboat by three!"

No-one complained and all passengers prepared themselves to leave. We patiently waited, buoyed by thoughts of reaching the shoreline latter in the day. But by three in the afternoon, the conditions worsened. We were forced to spend a cold and miserable night aboard the ship.

Mutinous Scoundrels

In the morning, the captain began similarly as before, "It is proposed to launch the lifeboats this afternoon. The seas will flatten and I'll have you on the mainland by three."

The crew were having none of this! "Launch the lifeboat now!" The failure of the captain to land the passengers and crew aroused much anger. Murmurings of incompetence spread like an infection. A short time after the captain's announcement, two crew broke open his cabin door. A third remained outside on guard.

But a horrible surprise awaited them. Behind a solid oaken desk, stood the captain and Cassanova. Each had a pistol in his hand; Cassanova was formerly attired in his Confederate officer's uniform. "Come in MATES, and close the door behind you," sneered the captain. "Is that you Pip outside my door?" he called, but received no answer. No, it wasn't Pip, but it may well have been.

In front of the captain lay a fortune in gold and silver coins. Cass immediately piped up with his nonsense, "The king is in his counting house, counting all his money."

But there is only so much of this rubbish one can tolerate. In reply to the nonsense, the mutinous crew member inquired, "I see Delila's fortune but where is Delila? Can we look yonder in your cupboard captain?" Surely this was a low taunt which was associated with the many rumors circulating regarding Delila's disappearance.

Yes, certainly. The question struck a raw nerve. No further words were exchanged and the mutineers were roughly bound, gagged and confined in the partially flooded scullery. For several minutes they thumped loudly upon the bulkhead, then there was nothing.

Rats and a Sinking Ship

About an hour after the insurrection, the captain summoned us all to the quarter deck. Supporting him to his right with a loaded pistol was Cassanova. A delegation of three crew members approached him. One sailor, his arms covered in tattoos, spoke with a most disdainful sneer. "What have you done with our mates, captain?"

"They are relieved of duties. They are taking a nap!"

"So captain, when do we launch?"

But the captain remained obstinately resolute. "A change of plans. The lifeboat will not be launched today." Abuse and ridicule reigned. "But friends let it not be said that I am an unreasonable captain! You shall all stand on the beach by noon."

"And how will we reach the shore captain, flap our wings?" inquired the tattooed dissenter.

"Young Pip shall swim a line to the shore. All passengers shall be transported ashore on that line. Pip has been briefed on his assignment and is prepared to leave."

Pip stood apprehensively beside the captain. He was dressed in light clothing. A cork lifejacket was strapped around his upper body; a bowline cinched loosely with light cordage hung from his waist.

The captain proceeded to explain his proposal. "Pip will swim a light line to the shore. A heavier tow line has been attached to the end, and a lighter line to that. That heavier lifeline with a passenger attached will be pulled to the shore and then retrieved to heave further passengers landward."

Surely this confirmed the captain's devious intentions towards Pip? Such an outrageous request was met initially with silence. But then Charles flared up. "Captain, you can't expect a 12-year-old boy to swim 400 yards to the beach. That's inhuman. Why do you dislike young Pip so?"

"Because I can!" the tyrant sneered smugly.

Then Mr Strausen stepped to the fore. "Captain, as a first-class paying passenger I must protest. As you are aware, I have contributed financially to the success of this voyage. The purchase of 12 cork lifejackets being one such example. It is sheer lunacy to expect one so young to negotiate rocky shoals, and treacherous currents to the shore."

But the captain was not used to being challenged. "Pray tell Mr Strausen, how do you propose to see all ashore by noon."

"In the lifeboat sir."

"The swell is too big to launch the lifeboat. Could your wife board a lifeboat in this swell?"

"The swell worsens in the afternoon captain when the wind picks up," interrupted Charles, "and the sea mist will further complicate your ill-conceived plans. Your judgement is poor captain, if indeed you are a captain."

"You'll never launch my lifeboat," interjected the captain in a fit of fury and he pointed his revolver threateningly at Charles. Cass drew his sabre. Gone was his pretense, his nursery rhymes and nonsense.

Charles was not easily intimidated, "a drawn sword cannot be returned to its scabbard," he said, glaring at Cassanova who immediately averted his gaze.

The intensity of the situation was apparent. The captain's complexion had turned florid and his hands shook. Despite this standoff, Charles stepped to the fore.

"Enough of this time wasting," he blurted out impatiently, "Give me the rope Pip and I shall swim for the shore."

The captain fired off a shot above our heads, "No sir! You are in my employ. I shall not risk my first mate in the swell."

"But you willingly throw a twelve-year old to the lions?" snapped Charles.

The captain now incensed by this public ridicule, turned his anger on Marley. The lurcher, straying too close to the side of the ship bore the brunt of his pent-up anger. The captain thrust her so viciously with his leg that she toppled over the side. Charles was quick to follow and as the dog arose to the surface, Charlie had her in his arms as he descended.

"Then swim for it with your mongrel," said the captain. "But here's a dose of lead to take with you." He drew a deadly bead on Charles.

While Mr Strausen momentarily grappled with the captain, I threw a floatation ring across his line of fire. Though the captain fired off several rounds, they were poorly directed. Charles who had retrieved the floatation device, was rapidly swept beyond the captain's range of fire.

Through all this Cassanova said and did nothing. He remained at the captain's side, supportive of his actions, and with a mysterious agenda on his mind.

Making a Swim of It

Sensing the futility of this impasse, I declared that I would swim for the shore. The captain appeared content with this suggestion. He now appeared anxious to rid his ship of all passengers. Whether we landed dead or alive didn't concern him.

I donned a life jacket and attached Pip's lifeline around my waist. I hugged Margaret, reassuring her I'd be okay. And just as I prepared to plummet into the surg, Pip came up to me. "Mr Treves, we could make a swim of it together?"

But the captain was immediate in ending honorable suggestions. "Back off lad, you are in my employ!"

After I plunged in, as with the first mate, the rolling breakers swept me towards the beach. Lying initially on my back, I watched the distance from the ship increase and on turning over, the distance to the shore close. And there was the first mate. He and his lurcher were safely on the shore waving jubilantly on the sandy cove.

But unlike Charles's unimpeded passage to the shore, mine was fraught with danger. My lifeline had become snagged on a shoal. I bobbed helplessly in the water. Further to my woes, I was being swept to the right, across from the sandy cove and towards the jagged cliff of the headland.

As the thunderous shore-break boomed onto the rocks, I heard two loud retorts from the boat. Had the captain shot someone?

That of course was not an immediate concern. Would they haul me back to the ship? Positive thoughts of salvation were fleeting; I had lost all faith in the captain. My mind flooded with despair. If I untied my lifeline I would end pummeled on the rocks. Nor could I survive here overnight. And what if the sharks arrived? Night temperatures would drop, the swell would increase and a sea mist would engulf me.

Suddenly, something brushed my shoulder. Fearing a shark, I reeled around in horror. "I told you we could make a swim of it." It was Pip. He had untangled the snagged towline. Assistance from passengers aboard the Sea Mist manoeuvred our lifeline adjacent to the sandy cove. The rolling breakers swept us shoreward and we jubilantly rejoined Charles and Marley.

The Tempest

Pip explained the revolver explosions. "He tried to shoot me similarly to how he fired at Charles. I suspect that Mr Strausen and Martha did their best to spoil his aim."

By late afternoon, a disheveled band of survivors huddled on the shore. The wind had freshened and the swell had picked up. Thanks to the foresight of Mr Strausen, we had provisions. Before leaving the stricken vessel, along with the help of others, he gathered these in one large wooden chest. There were several blankets, a pistol, flints, gunpowder, tea, biscuits, sugar, knives, plates, cups, candles, a lantern and compass. The swell swept the casket shore.

My Strausen's forethought arose in the hurley burley of the moment. Certainly, it was without the captain's sanction. And instantly upon the realizing this, the captain pumped six bullets into that chest endeavoring to send it to the bottom.

Our campsite was established under a stand of casuarinas. Their needles provided comfortable cushioning for our bedding. Their rotting needles served splendidly as tinder for a fire too. Casuarina wood generated strong heat, even when green. In the cities, they fueled bakers' ovens.

By 8 pm, the fiercest of gales erupted and we were forced into a sandstone cave. The cave had a towering overhang, much like a large verandah on a house. Such was the ferocity of the storm that we were forced inside the cave itself.

Huddled uncomfortably in its cold and rocky confines, we slept fitfully. Dingoes howled and the bush was alive with unsettling sounds.

Could there be tigers or bears in this new land? Marley's instinctive hunting skills saw her scurrying here and there for the best part of the night.

Uninvited Guests

We awoke to the warming rays of the sunshine and calm seas. Small amounts of debris were scattered across the beach. A glance seaward indicated that the Morning Mist had sunk. No masthead signified a resting place. The absence of wreckage indicated she had not broken up. She had slipped off the reef. The two adversaries lay nestled together on the ocean floor.

The loss of the ship signified different things to all of us. She had safely bore us through storms and calms over many months. Her sinking generally evoked feelings of loss and regret.

On the second day Pip, Charles and the Marley set out to forage for food. It was during their absence that our day turned horribly dark. Two shackled mutineers stumbled into camp herded by a drunken captain and Cass. Both were armed with revolvers. Bottles of rum jangled in a calico bag.

On entering our camp, the captain gazed around searchingly. Then blurting out in a drunken rage he said, "Show yourself Charles. Where are you Pip? I have a bullet here for you and that weevilly bag of bones."

At this particular point, I became fearful for Martha. Her intolerance for these 'turnips' as she called them, had reached flashpoint. I nestled closer to her to prevent an altercation. Not that I could restrain her. She weighed 200 pounds! Certainly, if the well-being of Bess or George was threatened, I had no doubt Martha would have launched herself at them. Whether they were armed, would not have mattered.

After learning that Charles was off foraging for food, they sat down by the fire. "Then we shall wait for them to return. Horribly drunk and impatient by midafternoon, the pair resorted to more devious measures. Beset upon making our lives difficult, the pair sacked our campsite. They extinguished our campfire with rocks and confiscated our weaponry and supplies.

They burdened us furthermore by leaving the two mutineers, both shackled, and hungry. And as the darkness closed, these misfits departed. The captain fired off one chilling admonishment. "Rest assured, you primates, you can count on us returning soon."

But there was good reason that Charles, Pip and the Marley did not return. In their drunken state our assailants failed to account for our numbers. When they first infiltrated our camp, there were 12. But after rummaging through our provisions, there were ten. I'd sent young George and Bess to the north to warn Charles. Several miles along the coast, they met up with Charles and warned them about the intruders.

After the captain departed, I followed him at a distance. It was simple to track two drunkards. Charles would be very interested in visiting their camp.

Charlie's Plan

The trauma generated by the captain's visit angered Charles. Regarding the theft of our possessions, he vowed to retrieve them. "I'll turn their day into a nightmare," he promised, "And I plan to do it soon!"

Charles greeted the mutineers warmly. Tank, the second mate was short and powerful. Igor was brute of a man who stood at over six feet. Both had served under Charles in several crossings of the Pacific. Both respected Charles as a leader.

Information passed on from the chained mutineers proved invaluable for us. Many questions were fired at them. Did you launch the lifeboat? Were you caught in the storm? Did you recover any provisions? Tank, answered most questions honestly.

"Dark threating clouds prompted the captain to load up the longboat and push forth into the increasing swell. The storm was quickly upon us and we were relentlessly swept towards the shore. One large wave overturned the boat dumping us onto the beach."

"What became of Delila's treasure?" I asked.

"No idea!" snapped the two simultaneously. Mr Strausen and I exchanged incredulous glances.

"We'll move camp tomorrow morning," instructed Charles who feared a return visit from the captain. "I'll show you a fortress, a veritable stronghold!"

We relocated in the morning. All approved of our new home. Charles introduced us to a multi – storied, conglomerate pillar, honeycombed with sea caves. It afforded us elevated views of the coastline to the north and south. I named it the Sentinel.

Immediately after our relocation, Charles planned to visit the captain's camp. But on the morning before he set out, Marley alerted us of imminent danger. Two men were approaching some 100 yards distant. Fearing the approach of the captain and Cass, we slunk into the shadowy confines of the Sentinel. Charles, undaunted by their arrival, strode out with Marley to welcome them.

The two men appeared completely spent. Unshaven, pathetic, and in raggedy garments, they posed no threat. Collapsing on their knees, they pleaded for assistance. "Help us please."

"Who are you?" Charles inquired.

"Survivors from the Esperalda." Immediately Charles wrapped an arm around each and assisted them to the Sentinel.

Our numbers had grown by four over several days. Two were in chains and two were in poor health and spirits. With our provisions almost exhausted, Charles was determined to raid the captain's camp today.

Charles and Pip had barely left the camp when five Indigenous people visited us. They placed a large piece of bark on the rocks adjacent to the Sentinel. Fearful of each other, no conversation was made between us and the warriors. There was whole fish, some bulbous yams, rock lilies, native grapes, and burrawangs, a type of cycad. The padre at the mission later taught me the names of all those bush foods.

The Aboriginal warriors left us flavored water in an animal skin bound together with animal sinews. It was flavored by the blossoms of the grass trees and paper bark.

Strangely we never saw any of that group again. It appeared as though the dense rainforest had swallowed them up.

In our hungry, weakened states, the delicacies were wholeheartedly appreciated. Food gathering parties were dispatched daily to gather the same. This decision nearly cost us our lives!

The Raiding Party

Tank openly described the setup of the captain's camp to Charles. "Climb up the ridge near the shipwreck for fifty yards. You'll see their campsite below. They'll start drinking at two in the afternoon. By five they'll be rolling drunk." Charles followed these instructions to the letter, and at five, he descended into their camp.

As Marley shadowed Charles everywhere, there was no keeping them apart. For that reason, Pip was a necessary requirement on the raid. He restrained Marley while Charles tampered with the provisions. The two felons lay in a drunken stupor for the entire period of our visit.

Charles loaded an assortment of supplies into a large calico bag. A chisel, hammer, gunpowder, flintstone and candles were readily accumulated. Into the empty bags from which he had pilfered oatmeal, rice, tea and sugar, Charles placed shells, sand and pebbles. He emptied selected bottles of rum into the surf and refilled them with seawater and sand.

Charles noted the lifeboat in good condition. To block their escape, he confiscated the oars and rejoined Pip. A full moon facilitated their safe return to our camp.

Bush Tucker

Immediately after the raid of the captain's camp, Charlie, Pip and Marley set out to climb the central plateau. That night, they did not return. After one night we were worried; a second nights' absence caused much consternation. Charles and Pip returned on the third evening. They'd climbed onto the plateau where they found a foundling mission occupied by a padre and 20 children. Several miles further to the south they stumbled upon a leper colony, eking out a living in basalt caverns.

They'd also traversed partly along the road to the stagecoach changing station at the river. And though Charles and Pip were buoyant about a return to civilization, they found us uncaring and uninterested in their discoveries. Some life-threatening ailment had descended upon us! Severe vomiting, malaise, headaches and stomach cramps plagued us. Martha and Bess alone appeared immune. These two angels of mercy tended to our needs as we lay helplessly on our beds. We had no appetite and could tolerate only small amounts of water.

Careful detective work was required to work out the cause of our sickness. Four of us were unaffected. Martha and Bess suspected that the burrawangs were the culprit. The undulating slopes around the Sentinel were littered with them. Their pulped fruit was one delicacy provided by the Indigenous warriors. Martha and Beth had not eaten the fruit. Nor had Pip and Charles who were busy exploring the terrain. What we had failed to recognize was that Aboriginal people soaked the white pulp in water for one week. This leached out the poisons. We, on the other hand, pulped it and immediately ate it!

Though we learnt about this preparation years after, our suspicions about the plants were sufficient to exclude them immediately from our diet.[4]

During our slow recuperation, Marley supplemented our diet with possums. Oysters were readily available. With the fishing line retrieved from the captain's camp, I caught regular supplies of flathead and bream.

Several of our group raised our lagging spirits by designing quaint little hats from the fronds of the cabbage palm tree. From the whale carcasses thrust up on the beach, intricate designs were carved in the bone. This was termed scrimshaw.

During our convalescence Charles empathized the need to climb onto the great plateau and hence back to civilization.

---

[4] This curious plant, as I would later find out was the most common of 11 species in NSW. These plants are the most primitive seed-bearing plants, and the most commonly occurring and widely spread cycad in NSW. They are the most southerly occurring cycad in the world and can tolerate minus degree temperatures; they enjoy a long life of over one hundred years. Early pioneers used the fronds as padding in couches and mattresses. The tight clusters of plants are the haunts of a range of animals ie foxes, feral cats, lyrebirds and small mammals. Starch was extracted from burrawangs for laundry purposes. Residues were used for adhesive paste.

A wide assortment of birds and small
mammals' nest in the burrawangs.

Gathering Storm Clouds

During Charles's absence, the group's dynamics changed noticeably. Crew members from the Esperalda and Morning Mist spent much time together. Their uninvited invasions into the quarters of others caused unrest. The Sentinel was comprised of a maze of caverns. These served splendidly as cabins in a ship. We fashioned comfortable beds out of seaweed or needles from the casuarina trees. Bess and several other ladies were mostly targeted by the crew. Martha did her best to ensure their privacy and loudly voiced her disapproval.

Igor, the largest of the Esperanza's survivors took a liking for Bess. He frequented the cavern where she was accommodated. This led to altercations with Martha and also George who was physically outmatched against the brute.

When Igor brushed George aside as one does an annoying insect, a serious conflagration loomed. The timely intervention of Mr Strausen and I prevented further escalation.

Trouble again arose after Charles and Pip returned from their exploration. When Igor cornered the young couple, Martha appeared quickly on the scene. Igor twisted her arm awkwardly. "Go and change your apron grandma."

"Unhand me you wretch," Martha screamed. But such defiance only enraged the brute. At this point Charles appeared. "Have we a problem Martha?"

"No problem, Charlie – boy," quipped Igor, and he departed. Charles's exploits at the wharves were well known. Always keen to defend the underdog, his reputation was legendary.

But Charles carefully noted this incident. Igor was a troublemaker and he may have to deal with him further down the line.

The Captain's Final Command

By the time we had recovered from the effects of the burrawangs, our provisions had dropped alarmingly low. We were forced further and further from the settlement for sustenance.

Forage parties were organized and fragmented into three. One group, which I will refer to as the seamen clique, insisted on foraging to the south in the direction of the captain's camp. This rather dubious band, which included the Esperalda's survivors, and the crew members, returned to camp smelling of rum!

An alarm was raised one morning when it was found that the crew had broken camp. "They've taken the oars!" Pip reported.

Charles, Pip, Marley and I immediately headed in that direction. As we rounded the headland, we witnessed an unbelievable sight. The captain and Cass had their revolvers trained on seamen who were carrying a large treasure chest and the oars.

Under the supervision of the captain, the boat was dragged into the surf. The chest was loaded aboard. Tank and Igor sat abreast ready to row. The two survivors from the Esperalda were invited to run for their lives. Both zigged and zagged and although several shots were fired off in their direction, none found their mark. Out past the breakers they rowed, out towards the sinister reef which I had named Black Rock.

Then a curious event occurred. The boat was raised up and overturned. The four occupants floundered momentarily and disappeared. No-one made it safely back to shore.

When we arrived on the beach, two desperate men collapsed in the sand. They were badly shaken and willingly gabbled on about the incident.

"Tank and his Igor had shown us where the treasure was hidden. When attempting to steal this the captain apprehended us.

"He offered us a reprieve. If we could steal the oars, we could share the treasure. This we agreed to do. The captain sealed the deal with a tote of rum. As the captain and Cass guzzled from several bottles, they began to gag and vomit. The bottles contained sandy salt water.

"The captain in his drunken state blamed us for this incident along with the calico bags filled with shells and sand! He claimed that we were spying for Charles and the ship-wrecked survivors at the camp."

The Landslide

With our provisions exhausted, and with an urgent desire to mingle again with other folk, we prepared to climb onto the plateau. In what resembled a long daisy chain, Charles had roped us together, interspersing the confident and lesser endowed climbers amongst one another.

The Devil's Archway was the first formidable obstacle that we were forced to climb. Beneath this imposing land bridge, a treacherous current swirled. I named this the Maelstrom.

Twenty minutes into the climb, Charles sent us scurrying for protection behind the trees and boulders. "Rockslide," he shouted. Here at this treacherous washaway, a long trail of scree trailed a hundred yards down to the creek bed. We watched several large rocks erupt over the edge, gathering momentum, rocketing down the slope and demolishing several grasstrees and casuarinas far below. A fearful silence prevailed. All progress halted.

Suddenly, from over the rise immediately above, two teenage boys appeared from the mission. Charles and Pip recognized them immediately. "We had spoken with them several days before when visiting the mission," said Pip. "Their names were Mut and Jeff. Strange names for two boys? They are comic strip names. And Mut readily accepted being labelled as the dog."

The teenagers moved with frantic urgency, quite oblivious about any landslide that could have resulted in tragedy. "Please help us," Jeff garbled, "The Devil has placed a curse on the twins! He wants them in the underworld. He's turned their bodies scarlet. Their tongues are white and covered with red spots."

"They are symptoms of Scarlet Fever," claimed Margaret. "We must attend them."

Charles doubted that would happen. "The rockslide has terrified our group. There's talk about a return to the Sentinel. I doubt whether we'll reach the escarpment."

"We'll have you at the mission within the hour," added Mutt.

And such was their confidence, we agreed to follow them. They took us down the slope momentarily and up another ridge. It proved far less perilous, and we reached the mission in less than an hour.

As we approached, the distraught padre wailed inconsolably, "The Devil is in our midst. He's taking my children to the underworld!"

Martha and Margaret requested to examine the boys immediately. I was concerned for her but she had set about diagnosing the patients. I hugged her reassuringly as if she was embarking on a long sea voyage. Thoughts of our children flooded back to me at this time.

As the ladies entered into the mission, Charles and Pip, paraded around the grounds ever watchful that a devil may be lurking there. The remainder of the group nestled down in the coolness of a kurrajong tree where we waited for Martha and Margaret to return.

An hour after the ladies disappeared into the mission, a restrained padre appeared again. He welcomed us inside where we were treated to lemonade and damper.

Very much aware of our eagerness to return to civilization, the kindly old padre offered the services of his boundary rider. "Old Brummy will lead you to the crossroads at the river. From there a coachline will convey you to Sydney."

These words were manna from heaven! We all eagerly sought to reacquaint ourselves with civilization again. For Charles, it meant answering the irresistible call of the sea. Marley, of course, was content to follow him anywhere. And Charles was not inclined to part ways with his loyal companion.

As most passengers were unable to afford overland coach fares, Mr Strausen insisted on footing the bill. That includes Marley, "It is the very least we can do to repay you both for your service."

"Three cheers for Isador, Charlie and the lurcher."

Now whereas this news held great appeal for us all, Margaret's later announcement was far less so. "The boys are at a low ebb. It would be inhuman to abandon them. We will remain here and tend to their needs. Isolation, broth, bed care and Epsom Salts should aid their recovery over several weeks."

Certainly, this was met with varying degrees of concern. For me it was quite disturbing; I was to be separated from Margaret. And most of us had grown very fond of Martha. None more so than George and Bess.

Old Brummy the Boundary Rider

At first light, the kindly old padre emerged out of the mist. Behind him materialized a horseman. Both horse and horseman appeared connected to the other. Both appeared noticeably weathered from the elements, and both exuded a wearisome demeanor, as if they had seen the best and worst that life had to offer. Old Brummy had a persistent hacking cough.

He tipped his hat to us; that was the extent of his animation. The swarms of flies annoyed Patches his old nag more than they did Brummy. The old nag swished his tail, stamped his foot, and whinnied in annoyance.

"Brummy has insisted on escorting you to the crossroads," said the padre. "He's a quiet companion but his loyalty is beyond doubt. He'll guide you safely to the staging station. He'll defend you to the death if necessary."

A group of battle-fatigued travelers assembled for our sojourn to Sydney. But there were positive, buoyant signs too. What fine apparel would we find in the shops at Sydney Town? I farewelled Margaret and promised to return in seven days.

Like the body and tail of a serpent, we snaked along the mountain ridge. Old Brummy and his steed were the head; the rag-tag wearisome assortment of survivors, the body and tail.

An hour from the mission we gazed down upon a picturesque vista of the river far below. And even as we luxuriated in the scenery, something caused Brummy concern. Several hundred yards down the slope he halted.

"There are bushrangers on the river," he drawled. "They're headed this way. It's best to avoid an engagement." Brummy stopped beside a rocky outcrop. "It will conceal our tracks," he said. But even these few words were punctuated by that hacking cough.

We trampled for twenty yards into the bush and sheltered behind a stand of grasstrees. These iconic wonderments loomed as green haired, terrestrial warriors with spear-like armaments.

Brummy had two pistols in his belt. He handed Charles his sabre.

After what appeared as an eternity, six horsemen trailed up the hill. They presented as a disheveled horde, their belts bristled with armaments. The leader was clearly in control. His band trailed subserviently behind.

As if possessing a sixth sense, the leader stopped adjacent to where we had entered the bush. Had he heard us? Had he seen our tracks? "Brummy, I thought I told you to see a doctor!" Brummy said nothing, but rose to his feet, untethered his horse and moved out in view of the bushrangers. He signaled for us to remain, particularly Charles who had drawn the sabre and was prepared to fight.

Just as Brummy reached the bushrangers, two thoroughly evil looking rogues galloped up to the group. Both smiled wickedly at Brummy, their broken and diseased teeth prominent, their greasy, mattered hair flailing wildly behind. Brummy was noticeably fearful of these two and moved towards the leader for protection. "I'll end his suffering with one bullet," the short, stouter fellow offered. That was Curley Bill, and his partner was Stretch McGaw. Immediately this dim-witted mate drawled, "Why waste a bullet?" And unsheathing his sabre, he raised it above Old Brummy's head.

But the head bushranger asserted his leadership, "Leave Brummy alone!" And he signaled his group to move up the rise. But as Curley Bill and his associate drew abreast of Brummy, they spat contemptuously in the old man's face.

Seemingly unaffected by the insolence, Brummy returned to us. After rejoining the track, he led us onward to the staging station. This incident affected us all gravely and we barely said a word until we reached the river. Brummy, as mentioned, didn't appear fazed, but that persistent cough was a worry. It appeared to be worsening.

The Obnoxious Coach Driver

Brummy delivered us safely to the staging station by the river. What an experience. Staging stations were established approximately 15 miles along the coach lines. Here fresh horses were harnessed and the coach continued on its journey. Some stations offered refreshments. Not so in this case. Here a father and his nine-year-old son attempted to run a business. They lived in a bark roofed humpy supported by four poles. There were no glass windows; the walls were sacking; the door was comprised of packing cases. The area was roughly fenced with saplings. Inside this were 10 horses nibbling away at scant pickings.

"Do the bushrangers trouble you?" Charles inquired of the father.

"The leader is a good fellow. He provides us with provisions and stray horses. But the two rogues who ride with him would do us great harm if given the opportunity. Benjamin, their leader keeps them on a short leash."

"Then I hope they remain on that leash." I told him. "Good luck to you and your boy."

"Thanks mister. My son and I are both prepared for trouble. Ben kindly supplied us with two revolvers and ammunition."

While waiting for the horses to be hitched, we cooled ourselves in the shallows beneath the casuarinas. Suddenly, an abrupt and abrasive driver hustled us aboard. But as Charles and his dog approached, he screwed up his face as if he'd swallowed a lemon. "Is that a lurch?" And on receiving a nod from Charles, he reached down for his shot gun. "Dogs aren't paying passengers."

"This one pays double," said Mr Strausen. But the obstinate driver was having none of it. "No lurch will ever climb onto my coach."

"Either both or none," replied Charles.

"Then it's none," sneered the driver.

"Then you miss out on three fares!" added Mr Strausen.

"You can make that four," said Pip, and he lined up behind Charles.

"Have it your own way," the driver snapped. "No stinking lurch is welcome here. You boy are a brat and you sir are a fool!" He pointed threateningly at each in turn. "This terrain is frequented by murderous bushrangers. The swamp teems with snakes, deadly tigers, browns and death adders. Enjoy your 25 mile walk."

But Charles was not fazed by the distance or the driver's spiteful scare mongering. And of course Pip and Marley would readily follow Charles through the Gates of Purgatory.

And as the coach lurched forward, Charles drew abreast of the driver. "I knew a sea captain like you. Obnoxious and insolent. I'll gleefully choose a dog and boy's company to yours. Count on me looking you up in Sydney Town."

Charles's intimidatory taunt appeared to faze the driver. With reins in his hand and without his shotgun, all the wind suddenly dissipated from the driver's sails; all the blood drained from his face. Whipping the horses viciously, the coach sped off leaving our beloved companions enveloped in a thick plume of dust. Dispirited and disconsolate we waved until they disappeared from sight.

In an attempt to raise our spirits, Isador declared, "We're meeting them on Tuesday near the tall ships. I'm treating you all to lunch on the harbour."

"Shall we invite our driver?" queried George. "Charles would so appreciate meeting him again."

"But not with that shot gun!" I added

Old Sydney Town

Our party was quickly absorbed into the hurley burley of Sydney Town. Most of which I never saw again. Not so Bess and George, for they annually visited Martha who eventually took up residence at Tumby. I saw Charles regularly. On our first meeting he clasped his powerful arms around me as a father welcomes a prodigal son. Marley had not forgotten me. She leapt up to her full height, her front paws on my shoulders. Her momentum knocked me backward into Charlie's arms. And Pip was the respectful young gentleman who I had learnt to admire. "Nice to see you again Mr Treves."

Charles was cock-a-hoop about having secured a berth on a schooner for America the following week. Marley would accompany him. She was adjudged a welcoming distraction for passengers and crew on a prolonged voyage. Isador Strausen played a significant role in Charle's posting. He provided an impeccable reference. His captain was a seasoned and respected leader. Like several other sea- farers he had an ivory leg, a legacy of skirmishes with whales.

Mr Strausen had been busy organizing employment for Pip too. He spoke in glowing terms of the lad's courage, loyalty and dedication to his duties.

The Strausens did much to make my stay enjoyable in Sydney Town. Comfortable lodgings and exquisite meals were a feature of their generosity. In their gracious company I attended numerous social outings. They accompanied me to garden parties, church services, river cruises and afternoon teas. Though always welcoming, I felt uncomfortable fitting into their affluent lifestyle. After such gratitude, it was with reluctance that I revealed my intentions of returning to Tumby. I had an irrepressible desire to return to my wife.

Both had anticipated this. "We have booked your return passage back to Tumby," John announced.

"What could I say?" With tears rolling down my cheeks I embraced them both and said nothing more on the subject.

On the morning of my departure, Charles, Marley and the Strausens came to say farewell. The Strausens gave me a parcel of supplies. It contained cheeses, cakes, and confectionary for the children. Charles and Pip presented me with a golden chain. It was attached to an ornate whalebone medallion. It featured a breeching blue whale. Charlie had never forgotten about my fondness for these noble creatures of the sea. "May it remind you of your good mates forever."

I wore that lucky charm around my neck unto my death.

Though Pip had sailed on his new venture, he had dearly wished to say farewell. But such are the fortunes in our lives. I never saw the Strausens, Pip, Charlie or Marley again.

A Letter from Abroad

During my short visit to Sydney Town, the police gave me a letter from England. Written four years previously, it finally caught up to me in Sydney. It was from my brother Richard Treves, an imminent English surgeon. I was overjoyed to hear that he had been knighted for services to medicine and humanity.

Prominent amongst his accolades was his friendship with the Elephant Man, John Merrick. From the age of five, John's body had begun to deteriorate. He'd a displaced hip and walked with a limp; his speech was barely intelligible; his right arm was deformed; and his hand was shaped as a web. His head had bulbous growths on it and he was unable to lie down.

John worked at a freak show when 21. As a caring benefactor, my brother Richard, organized permanent lodging at the hospital. He introduced John to the refined, well-to-do ladies of the English society.

John died at 27 years from asphyxiation while trying to lay flat on a bed like a human being.

John Merrick, a public domain photograph taken in 1898.

Night Passage

My return to the mission was the most memorable feature of my sojourn to Sydney. Whereas several Chinese, Aboriginals and two married couples opted to ride inside the coach, I elected to travel in Cobb's Box with the Tiny Montgomery, the driver. He was a man mountain, weighing at least 300 pounds? "Why do they call you Tiny?" I asked him.

"My four brothers weigh 400 pounds."

Besides he said, "My brother is called Curley; he hasn't a single hair on his head" Tiny was both a tour guide and raconteur.

He described the terrain and its colorful history as we sped through it. Tiny explained how the Aboriginals used the flower stems of grasstrees for spear shafts, and as a soft wood for lighting fires. Hard wood twirled rapidly in softwoods produced heat and a flame.

Tiny told me about Old Brummy too. The padre at the Mission employed him as a boundary rider when he was 16. His parents had been murdered by rampaging convicts.

The padre and Old Brummy enjoyed a father/son relationship. Brummy worked with the padre for thirty years. He resided in a bark hut behind the mission. And the padre gave him his horse Patches. All three were intensely loyal to each other.

Night travel was a feature of my coach ride. The early coaches which preceded Cobb and Co, had no lanterns illuminating the roadway. An Aboriginal warrior running before our coach with a firestick satisfactorily served in that role. And as there was no relief runner available at the next staging station, that same runner continued another 15 miles until he was relieved at the next station.

Tiny conjured up exciting action scenes, closely akin to the imagery in Henry Lawson's poem, The Lights of Cobb and Co. This was published around 25 years after my eventful return to the mission.

Swift scramble up the siding where teams climb inch by inch.
Pause bird-like on the summit-then breakneck down the pinch.
Past haunted half-way houses where convicts made the bricks,
Scrub yards and new bark shanties, we dash with five or six.
Through stringybark and blue gum and box and pine we go.
New camps are stretching across the plains,
the routes of Cobb and Co.[5]

At first light our team struggled to climb a steep incline. Tiny ordered us to walk before the coach to the summit. On this occasion, two notorious bushrangers lay awaiting. Who could forget Curley-Bill and Stretch Mc Neil? I instantly recognized them from their altercation with Old Brummy. Rifling through our possessions, they confiscated our weapons and valuables.

Curley, the uncouth and rancid smelling beast, proceeded to harass the young women. This was not appreciated by their husbands who were instanty bludgeoned to the ground. When Tiny intervened, a rusted sabre was levelled at his throat.

Amidst this chaos, the remaining members of the bush-ranging horde burst upon the scene. In a wild fury, Benjamin charged his horse

---

[5] A public domain poem. Henry Lawson's fine work, The Lights of Cobb and Co was published late in the 19th century. Cobb and Co was an American coaching company which flourished in Australia during the second half of the nineteenth century.

at Curley, knocking him to the ground. "Don't molest the passengers! What part of that rule don't you understand?" he bellowed.

Stretch helped a heavily concussed Curley onto his horse, and in a short period the horde galloped off. No words were exchanged and no possessions were returned.

That steep incline which caused us distress going up, proved equally disturbing going down. Our brakes failed! Though brake failure had resulted in the deaths of several drivers, Tiny proved himself more than capable in the situation. Strangely in our instance, he whipped the horses to make them gallop faster. To allow a runaway coach to strike the polars often resulted in them bolting frantically away at breakneck speed. [6]

Tiny saw me safely to the staging station at the crossroads. The horses were changed and after farewelling Tiny with three cheers, I made my way slowly towards the mission.

---

[6] The two horses harnessed closest to the coach.

A Search for Old Brummy

My arrival at the mission was not as I had anticipated. Margaret approached me horribly distressed. "Jon. Listen closely. Brummy coughed up blood last night. This morning he has disappeared. The padre is beside himself. I am fearful for both."

"Is Patches in the stable?"

"No! Jon you must find him. He is need of urgent medical care." Search as I might for two days, no trace of Brummy was found. For six months we heard nothing.

Then a band of Aboriginal warriors approached the padre, indicating through sign language, that they had found Brummy's horse. I set off with them to retrieve him. For two days we hiked through the maze of gullies and ridges. The warriors sustained me with bush cherries, plums and dried fish.

Late in the second afternoon we located Patches. His mane was tangled with prickles and burrs, and his ribs threatened to burst through his skin.

The loyal old horse led us to the very bottom of a sheer cliff-face. There curled on his saddle cloth was the decomposing body of Brummy.

Not having any digging implements, I excavated the ground with a large flat piece of shale. I heaped a rocky cairn over the long serving boundary rider. The old horse appeared content that this was a reverent and honorable mark of respect. Patches sauntered over to the grave, nuzzling the rocks and whinnying pitifully.

But that old horse had no interest in returning home with me. And although I frequently glanced around expectantly in the hope he may be following, he never did. Content he was to live out his remaining days with his old mate.

Though the padre had long resigned himself to Brummy's death, the horse's reluctance to return to the mission was incomprehensible. "Where is Patches? Why hasn't he returned to his home?" I had no answer to these heart-wrenching pleas.

In that respect Margaret came to my assistance. Sensing the padre's distress, and with one arm cradling his waist, she led him outside to a large kurrajong tree. She bade him sit down on a large rock decorated with lichens. And in this natural setting she read him a verse from a poem. It was called Marshall's Mate and it bore direct reference to Brummy and his faithful horse Patches.

And now way out on Dingo Creek, when winter days are late,
The bushmen talk of Crowbar's horse a looking for his mate.
Beyond the Land of Break-of-Day and Sunset and the Dawn,
The souls of Crowbar and Crowbar's mate have gone.
Unto that Loving Laughing Land where life is fresh and clean,
Where rivers flow all summer, and the grass is always green. [7]

After the reading, without uttering one sound, the old padre rose to his feet and strolled into the mission. He moved in a way suggesting that a great burden had been lifted off his shoulders. Margaret and I both believed that in the poem the padre had found peace and reconciliation.

____

[7] Henry Lawson's poem Marshall's Mate published in 1894. Public Domain.

The Ebb and Flow of Fortunes

My return from Sydney was a period of great unrest. In the words of Charles Dickens, it was the best of times; it was the worst of times. It was the age of foolishness; it was the age of wisdom. It was the age of light; it was the age of darkness.

Whereas the loss of Brummy and his horse caused great upheaval particularly for the padre, this was offset by the rapid recovery of twins Joshua and Joseph. Do those names have a familiar ring for you? Yes, they were the names of our boys murdered by Quantrill at Lawrence.

During the boys' convalescence, Margaret cultivated a loving relationship with them, as they did with her. As the boys were abandoned and unnamed on the steps of the mission, no official names were bestowed upon them. In my absence at Sydney, the padre and Martha were complicit in naming them after our deceased twins.

Margaret and Martha alternated between nursing the twins at the mission and the lepers at the colony. During this time, a romance blossomed between Martha and a leper called Peter. The two later married and raised two children.

As a consequence of the ladies' regular attendance at the leper colony, (and I never once suggested this to either of them,) Joshua and Joseph contracted leprosy. The padre had no option but to refer them to the leper colony. This lay about 12 miles distant in the volcanic caverns.

During this period of upheaval, a savage storm flung the brigantine, Celeste contemptuously up on the beach at Sandy Cove. Again, the padre exerted strong influence towards repaying Margaret and I for our services. Over a period of two weeks, the wreckage of that ship was laboriously relocated up the steep escarpment. A beautiful little cottage was constructed for us. Beautiful panels of polished cedar adorned our little home.

The cottage commanded beautiful vistas of the coastline to the south and north. Here we lived contentedly for one year. During that time, Margaret who had a liking for English, contributed much towards both the twins' education and that of Peter too.

High up on the mountain ridge a shanty was
built for Jon and Margaret Treves.

But then the very bottom fell out of my world. Margaret's prolonged contact with the disease, saw her contract leprosy and quickly pass away. Such was my grief, I have not wished to elaborate on the heart wrenching details of her sad demise.

Dearest Margaret was laid to rest at the mission. A weekly service was conducted by the padre with all foundlings and lepers present. The grave was sculptured with weathered sandstone and regularly adorned with wildflowers.

From this setback, I plummeted into a deep and dark chasm from which I felt I would never return.

Rubbing Salt in a Wound

But there seemed no end to the bad news. The death of my dear wife was exacerbated by a letter from overseas. Our good friends the Strausens had perished at sea. On April 14th 1898, the Titan struck an iceberg in the Atlantic Ocean. When the first-class passenger, Ida was ushered into a lifeboat, she refused to leave her husband. When the attendant suggested that allowances could be made for such a kindly gentleman in the lifeboat, he insisted on remaining with the men. Then clasping her husband's arm tightly, Ida said, "I have spent a lifetime with my husband, I do not choose to leave him now."

The couple were swept off the deck as the ship floundered. Their bodies were located and they were buried together.

Such an honorable deed was widely heralded in America. At least four memorials were established in reverence to the pair. This inspirational biblical verse glorifies the magnificence of that event today. "Lovely and pleasant they were in their lives and in death they were not divided." Samuel 1:23

The Strausen's unfailing love and devotion for each other, burns brightly as a beacon still to this day.[8]

---

[8] The fictional deaths of Ida and Isidor Strausen mirrored the authentic deaths of the devoted couple Ida and Isidor Straus on the Titanic some twelve years afterward.
The loss of the Titan, an imaginary ship, was a novel by Morgan Robertson called 'Futility' written in 1898. It closely resembled the loss of the Titanic some 12 years after. The liners were of similar dimensions, the largest ship of its type in the world. Both faltered on an iceberg with insufficient lifeboats aboard. An appalling number of deaths resulted in both instances in the frig waters of the North Atlantic.

The Sentinel

Whereas the story to this point has been narrated by Jon Treves the fisherman, hereafter it is expedient to write in the third person and write about him.

After the death of his Margaret, Jon Treves remained on the craggy, windswept coastline. On stormy nights, when the ocean beat mercilessly into the cliffs below, he lay awake in his bed. "Nothing is as powerful as the wind," he said, "and the sea is her servant." Jon spoke loudly, as though Margaret was still with him. For ten years he had continued with this pretense.

"Life is very cruel," mused Jon whenever he thought of his wife's sad demise. She had died from the very disease she had chosen to treat.

Mostly, the old man's thoughts were pleasant. "Life can be kind and caring," he said again quite loudly. From their charitable work at both the leper colony and the mission, they had derived much pleasure and fulfilment.

After violent storms, many stately vessels had foundered on Black Rock. Barques, brigantines, and schooners lay upon the ocean floor with gaping holes in their hulls. This treacherous reef lay close to where he fished.

On most mornings, Jon wound down a precipitous pathway from his home with his rod slung over his shoulder. At the water's edge, he crossed the narrow land bridge. In fair weather, even when the tide was full and the water lapped each end of the arched causeway, he made the crossing. But when fierce winds prevailed and thunderous waves pummeled it, a great anxiety welled up inside him. Such were the conditions when the ships were dashed upon the rocks; such were the murderous conditions when the sailors were drowned. John sensed horror and dread in the dark swirling water beneath the Devil's Causeway. He named it the Maelstrom. During such times, he never risked a crossing, choosing instead to pass through a mosquito-infested swamp of treacherous quicksand.

At the bottom of this path, an immense column of conglomerate rose out of the sea. It looked like a clenched hand pointing defiantly to the sky. Jon called it the Sentinel, and it was special to him. It contained a network of sea caves. Here the old man moored his skiff.

The fisherman drew strength and endurance from the Sentinel.

Onward past the monolith, he crossed a flat platform. Upon this, the ocean's spume continually splattered, sounding similar to a fisherman's hand net cast into the sea.

The rocky platform was cut by glaring crevices. Through these, the ocean rumbled and gurgled into the sea caves beneath. From here wreckage for his house was salvaged. From here too he had plucked survivors from the sea. Precious few, however, had made the shore. The old fisherman wrapped the less fortunate souls in sailcloth and buried them in the sandy cove.

The sea caves were sacred to the old man, for he believed that the remains of seamen lay entombed there. Each morning, as he stood above them, he bowed his head and respectfully crossed himself. The good padre at the mission had instructed him so.

Into the open sea, well away from where he imagined the seafarers lay, he cast his rod. Here he caught many fine fish. Some he delivered to the leper colony, the oil of the salmon providing relief from their disease.

The Great Plateau

Sojourns to the leper colony and the mission were not without considerable danger. First, there was the climb to the great plateau. He did this by way of a 20-foot wooden ladder, the rungs bound on tightly with rope lashing to two schooner masts. The old man called this Jacob's Ladder.

Climbing Jacob's Ladder for the aged fisherman
was fraught with danger.

The old man hauled his ocean's catch up the Great Walls of Troy in straw baskets. Once onto the plateau, he harnessed his donkey to a cart, both of which were confined in a paddock there.

The journey to the mission took a half day's journey, the leper colony a further half. His rickety cart and his aged donkey, Old Bill, trudged along a perilous route, an old, disused mining track. Several sections had been washed away, and the entourage was forced dangerously close to glaring precipices.

There were, of course, the bushrangers, of whose infamy you may have heard. Many nightmarish tales have been circulated about them. These outlaws lived in the old, abandoned ghost town. Nearby shafts cut deep into the mountains.

His passage through a narrow ravine, named the Devil's Craw, was particularly unnerving. Glimpses of distant figures on clifftops above assured him that he was being closely observed.

The Putrid Pit was a salient reminder of the bushrangers' barbarism. It lay strategically positioned inside the Devil's Craw. It was tantamount to the scent of a dog left on a post. Into and around this pit, the bushrangers threw their excrement and the bodies of those they had murdered.

The Devil's Craw had another fearsome reputation. After heavy rain, floodwater swept through this bottleneck at a frantic rate. The limestone caves that pockmarked the canyon walls offered no refuge, as these were quickly inundated by the raging torrent. Caves high up in the cliffs are strewn with driftwood and, in one instance, the splayed bodies of two unfortunates who sought shelter there.

The Pied Piper

To the mission, he carted fish for the score of homeless children. The old man, his donkey, and his cart approached from out of the mountains from a largely disused road that had fallen into disrepair. The orphans kept a silent vigil in its direction, for few apart from the old man risked either the terrain or the hordes of bushrangers who camped in the mountains.

When they realized it was the old fisherman approaching, a handful of children swung excitedly on the thick rope that tolled the large

mission bell. Jubilant peals and a multitude of voices resounded across the barren plain: "The old man is coming! The old man is coming!"

For the fisherman, the sudden eruption of boys in his direction was tantamount to a cavalry charge. They greeted him in various affectionate ways; the smaller children locked their arms tightly around his legs. As the procession drew closer to the mission, a padre passed the smallest orphan to the old man. Plainly he was invalid, though he was particularly special, for he instantly clasped his arms around the old man's neck. And with this orphan cradled in his arms, the Pied Piper led a long procession towards the mission. And what a captivating cavalcade it was! Several orphans led Old Bill, who usually had another mounted his back. Several boys clambered aboard the cart itself, and the remainder danced and skipped jubilantly behind. All were eventually swallowed inside the sunbaked brick mission, all except Old Bill, of course, who received firsthand care in the stables.

"The fisherman and Old Bill are coming!"

The smallest, crippled orphan was special to the old man.

The Meeting

This morning for the old man was no different to any other as he trudged slowly down the precipitous pathway to the ocean. But no, a beautiful merchild lay resting on a thick belt of kelp. The fierce currents had forced her to seek refuge there. As each wave swept past, her black hair flowed inward and then back out again as the wash returned to sea.

"How tall are the land folk!" she sighed to the seahorses, and the stately creatures nodded. Observing the old man more closely, she gasped in horror. "He has the great sickness!" She noted that his skin was wrinkled and blotched. Hers was silken and milky white. Merfolk simply did not age.

This concern for the old man was not typical of those from the kingdom; the hearts of the merfolk were hard and cruel.

As if spellbound, the merchild studied the old man intently as he retraced his steps home along the mountain path. Then, feeling sufficiently rested and finding that the strong currents had abated, she headed back towards Black Rock. The merfolk lived amongst a graveyard of sunken vessels.

"How tall are the land folk!" she sighed to the seahorses and they nodded in agreement.

The Kingdom of Mer

As she swam past the shimmering, ghostly galleons, she was roughly seized and dragged to a forbidden section of the kingdom. She was taken past mounds of heaped bones and through the burial grounds of the merfolk.

The merchild did not struggle but hung her head in shame, her long hair concealing her terror. Nor did she weep, for the merfolk cannot cry. Instead, she made a groaning sound, much like a trumpeter fish caught on a line.

Through a tall corridor of larger human skeletons, they dragged her. In the eye sockets, the slimy bodies of sea creatures squirmed. The long, narrow courtyard ended abruptly at the jawbone of a blue whale, and into its gaping mouth she was taken. This was the throne room of the merqueen. For the child, the surroundings appeared austere and daunting. Trophies of horrendous maritime tragedies were arranged as a macabre exhibition on the throne room.

The merchild was roughly accosted and dragged
to a forbidden section of the kingdom.

The Gallery of Horrors conjured the greatest fear and trepidation for the merchild. Seated on the seabed facing a longboat, lay the crumpled body of a woman. She was dressed as a clown in bright harlequin colours. A hideous death mask was affixed over her face. And may well she have appeared pained. Draped around her body was a heavily rusted anchor chain!

Close by this blood chilling spectacle was a longboat with four occupants inside. In the bow sat a wizened faced captain, recognizable by his hat, accoutrements and weaponry. Beside him was a man dressed as a confederate army officer. Curiously he had horns protruding out of his head and a long tail. And he held a little velvet collecting bag. A large chest brimming with golden and silver coins sat immediately before him and the captain. Two sailors were positioned at the stern, each with an oar in their hands. One's arms were lathered in tattoos; his mate was a man mountain.

The five figures in the display sat mesmerized as if gazing into a warming fire. But there was little warmth radiating there. Their greedy eyes were closely affixed on the brimming chest of treasure.

Beyond this sat the merqueen herself, a lone figure lounged upon a blue coral throne. Her eyes were affixed cruelly upon the merchild. Her wicked smile revealed sharp, vicious teeth.

To the child in her terror, this frightening creature appeared amazingly similar to herself. Her skin was very white. Unlike the child, there were no greyish streaks through the tail.

On each side of this creature, six merfolk materialized. Each was identical to the other and appeared sinister and threatening, as Roman praetorian guards must have been. Their hair was as black as the deepest holes in the ocean. Their tails were banded with seaweed and closely resembled the patterns on poisonous sea snakes.

The tyrant's fury initially targeted the mermen who had apprehended the child. "Why have you summoned me here?" she shrieked, and she flapped her tail menacingly from side to side. Contrary to the praetorian guard, these mermen had no banding on their tails and were obviously of a lower rank.

To the queen's demand, they remained silent initially, and then as if summoning courage, bleated in unison, "Land folk bad."

"And why are the land folk bad?" the merqueen demanded.

"They rob the ocean of its treasure."

Strangely they said this, for inside the gaping jawbone, immediately behind the queen, there was a chamber morbidly decorated with all types of land treasures. One may have been forgiven for thinking that the merfolk were the thieves. Sea chests, bells, cannons, wooden figureheads, barrels, anchors, and skeletons festooned the royal chambers.

The rants of the merqueen continued. "Why do you speak of land folk?" the queen demanded.

The merfolk swished their tails menacingly in a fashion similar to their leader, and with a frightening, toothy glare, they pointed accusingly at the merchild.

The cruel despot now turned her anger to the child. "And what do you know of the land folk?"

In reply to these raucous rants, the merchild attempted to explain, but being distraught, she was unable to do so. A clumsily garbled message served only to inflame her interrogator more. "The land folk are tall. They have a sickness."

"You stupid child," shrieked the merfolk queen, tossing her head arrogantly about, "You are unworthy of our kingdom. To be kind and caring is to be weak."

She gestured towards the guards, and the merchild was again manhandled and dragged from the room. "We must arrange another meeting with the land folk," she said, and she clapped her hands with delight.

"To be kind and caring is to be weak," scowled the merqueen.

A Good Samaritan

Two days after this distressing incident, as the fisherman trudged down the mountain path, his attention centered on the crazed behavior of the gulls. They wheeled frantically above, their raucous screams drowning out the breakers crashing on the shore. Sensing a great tragedy, such as a beached whale, he hurried down to the sea caves. There he found a beautiful merchild huddled and trembling uncontrollably. The fin of her tail had been cut away.

The merchild stared wide eyed in terror and groaned dreadfully like a little trumpeter fish caught on a line.

The old man stroked her matted hair, and such were his gentle ways that she allowed him to tend her wound. Fearing the voracious feeding habits of the gulls, the old man cradled the merchild in his arms and struggled up to his sanctuary. All the while, the cruel eyes of the merfolk queen burnt into him. "To be kind and caring is to be weak," she scowled contemptuously. With a certain assurance she said, "Soon, old man, your bones will decorate my palace."

And as macabre as this sounds, this was the obsession of the merqueen. For many years, the remains of seafarers had been gathered to decorate her chamber. Human bones were highly prized trophies throughout the merfolk kingdom!

"Soon old man, your bones will decorate my chamber."

Renewed Purpose

Each morning after this incident, the old man hustled down to the sea caves with greater purpose. He cut oysters from the rocks for the merchild's soup, and he caught yellowtail, a delicacy for all merfolk.

Collecting oysters and catching yellow tail for the merchild became one of the fisherman's favorite pastimes.

The old man pacified the merchild with stories of the sea. She lay enthralled, listening to tales of the great blue whales and their horrendous battles with giant squid. "The whale is the noblest creature in the ocean," he told her. "No sea creature cares for her infant more than a whale."

Above all, the child loved the stories of the orphans. Generally, her questions centered around the lame boy, the plucky little fellow who was wheeled around in a cart. He was the sole survivor from a frightful tempest. Though seriously injured, the old man was able to haul him miraculously from death's door. The little boy was special to the old man, and he loved him more than all others.

Stories about the lame orphan boy were the
favorites of the merchild.

The old man's stories had a calming effect on the merchild. They allayed the terrifying, evocative thoughts conjured from the merqueen's brutality. The child listened to his stories longingly and usually lapsed in a deep, restful sleep, resting her head on the old man's shoulder.

From their earliest time together the merchild called the old man 'Kind Fisherman' and the old man asked for nothing else. And he simply called her 'Child'. This may seem to readers as disappointing and unimaginative.

But the old man secretively believed his foundling to be a Selkie, a mysterious being from the sea. He felt that one day she would transform from a sea creature into a human. And each occasion he observed her sleeping restfully, he lovingly whispered, "Sweet dreams my Selkie Child." But never once did he call her 'Selkie Child' during her waking hours for good and bad tales had been spread about Selkies.

A large waterfall cascading down the mountain also aided in the merchild's rehabilitation. The cascade pooled near the old man's residence. For the foundling, it provided a cooling environment in which she could recover. The merchild's wound quickly healed, and the old man enjoyed his happiest times since the death of his wife.

The merchild grew increasingly anxious whenever the old man visited the sea caves. "Watch out for the merqueen," she warned.

Beware of the Merqueen

About a fortnight after the terrible event, the old man had a terrible sense of dread as he crossed the platform. He listened as the water gurgled into the sea caves. Gulls wheeled eerily overhead. On seeing no apparent danger, he cast forth his rod. Almost immediately, there was a vicious tug on the line. As he hauled it towards him, a beautiful girl of perhaps eighteen rose out of the water. Instantly, the old man knew who she was.

"Help me onto the rocks, old man." She smiled warmly and held a slender arm out for him. "I long to know more of the land folk and their ways."

But the old man saw cruelty in the creature's eyes, and in her wicked smile. He slunk back fearfully from the water's edge.

"Help me onto the rocks, old man, and these treasures are yours. They have been gathered from the deepest realms of my kingdom. I long dearly to learn about the land folk and their ways." The queen plucked a seaweed bag from her waist and threw it at his feet. An assortment of colored gemstones lay inside. But the old man did not attempt to pick them up. Again, he stepped back fearfully.

By now, the patience of the merqueen had been duly tried. Her enticing smile now turned horribly dark. "Foolish land folk!" she screamed.

Sloshing sounds from behind him alerted the old man to a more pressing threat. While she had distracted the old man, several hideous figures had now drawn dangerously close. They whirled little seaweed nets above their heads, grinning dreadfully with dagger-shaped teeth.

Closer and closer the mermen drew, and nearer and nearer the old man retreated towards the clutching grasp of the merqueen.

From the water hole high on the cliff, the merchild witnessed these events, and in her distress, she tumbled over the edge of the rock pool.

With a desperate sweep of her arm, the merqueen lunged at the old man. The old man's bulk clashed heavily against the merqueen, knocking her off balance. And into a narrow fissure, he momentarily eluded both the tyrant and her henchmen. Sloshing through knee-deep water, he waded deeper and deeper into a sea cave. Behind he heard the curses of the mermen as they floundered about in pursuit.

The old man passed his skiff and emerged from the crevice beside the Sentinel. Up onto this sanctuary he climbed. Here the merfolk could never reach him. He listened to the savage rebukes of the merqueen as she scolded them for their uselessness. He watched each creature plunge into the depths.

Here atop the Sentinel the old fisherman felt similarly to Quasimodo when he carried Esmeralda high into the cathedral at Notre Dame. "Sanctuary. Sanctuary," he called out to the merqueen."

For an indeterminable period, the old man sat recovering from this ordeal. His head swam, and his heart pounded. It was not until late afternoon that he felt well enough to climb back to his home. Such was his fatigue as he struggled along the precipitous path that he failed to notice the forlorn body of the merchild splayed out on the waterfall.

On finding no trace of her in his house, he slept fitfully, waking occasionally and calling out, "Selkie Child. Please answer me!".

It was not until late afternoon that he found her. She had seriously injured her back and was badly burnt by the sun. Once again, the old man cradled her as he trod up the pathway. There he tended her injuries.

For one year, the old man cared for the child. So severe were her injuries that she grew to depend on him. "What will become of you, child?" thought the old man. "For I grow old and weak."

Never once did he trouble the merchild with this concern. He would never return her to the kingdom, and the dry plain around the mission was too hot and exposed for a sea creature. "I will watch out for a sign," the old fisherman thought.

Deliverance

What may have initially appeared as a sign to the old fisherman, occurred just one week later. Old Bill died. The old donkey's thoughts of the old man were surely foremost in his mind to the last. They found Old Bill curled beside his old wagon. This was a sad loss for the fisherman. For ten years that plucky, stout- hearted little fellow had toiled without complaint.

Bill the boundary rider dug the old donkey's grave adjacent to his little wagon. The fisherman affixed a sign on a cross overshadowing that grave. "To dear Bill. Steadfast and resolute in all weather and mountainous terrain. Adored and remembered forever. Jon."

No, it wasn't the sign that the fisherman had sought, but it was a forerunner, a prelude. One week after, a terrifying storm thundered around the district. A devastating bolt of lightning struck the Sentinel, and the vegetation on the top lit up like a torch. The surrounding waters grew unusually calm. The old man watched these events carefully. Of all the storms he had witnessed, this was decidedly different. The old man wrapped the child in a blanket. "Our time has arrived, child," he told her.

"Where could we go in such a frightening storm?"

"To a better place."

As the old man struggled down the mountainside, his light-headedness returned, and he became breathless. On several occasions, he was forced to rest. Curiously, the lashing rain had abated, and the winds had ceased.

The lightning strikes persisted out towards Black Rock. The old man comforted the merchild, and she was quickly reassured by his calm manner.

He sought his skiff. It lay protected and unharmed in the sea cave. Laying the merchild carefully on its floorboards, he kissed her lovingly on the forehead. Then untying the mooring rope, he paddled out of the cave. Once outside, he unfurled the sail, and skillfully launched his skiff through the rocky shoals.

The fisherman glanced around the coastline which now loomed in darkened shadow. The Sentinel itself appeared resplendent and more formidable than ever. From this, the old man drew renewed determination and reassurance. Turning the tiller eastward, he headed into the blackness, out into the open sea into the direction of the receding storm.

The Sentinel appeared resplendent and more formidable than ever. From this, the fisherman drew determination and reassurance.

The fisherman headed into the blackness, into the open sea in the direction of the receding storm.

The HMAS Providence

"No sign of any life sir," shouted the lookout aboard the HMAS Providence. With great difficulty in the heavy swell, a line was secured from the schooner to the skiff.

"Both are dead, sir. The man is very old, and the other, ah, she is the most beautiful child that I have ever seen."

The captain shook his head. "Who would venture out on a night like last?"

"It is very odd, sir. There are no provisions aboard. And despite the ferocity of the storm, there is little water in the boat. The old man is cradling the child in his arms. She's fallen asleep with her head on his shoulder."

The sailor's intent to separate the pair was met by a quick and strong rebuke from the captain. "Leave them so," he ordered. "For they were happy together in life. Allow them to remain together in death."

When the bodies were brought aboard, the captain gasped with alarm. Kneeling down beside the fisherman, the tears welled in his eyes. He clasped the old man tightly in a fond embrace. On closer inspection he noticed the silver chain around the old man's neck. It was the beautiful whalebone scrimshaw depicting a huge blue whale breaching. A first-mate had given this gift to Jon Treves 30 years ago. Of course, that first mate was Charles the captain of the HMS Providence. Choking back the tears and speaking in a distressed and hardly audible fashion, he stammered, "It is Jon Treves the old fisherman from Tumby." And barely had he uttered the words, Jon Treves a tall handsome lad emerged from the gathering of bewildered crew. Initially, he stood reverently with his head bowed. It was the first mate Pip. And when Pip noted the gold chain and whalebone, he crouched down placing one hand on Charles and another on the fisherman. "Mr Treves I always knew we could make a swim of it,"

Immediately the fondest memories flooded back through their minds, smoldering images of Isador and Ida Strausen, Marley, Margaret Treves, Martha and the kindly padre at the mission. Most had passed away now, but many of the richest and the finest memories remained.

For many years, Charles had followed the career of this selfless man and his good works with the poor and disadvantaged. Immediately, as a mark of respect, the captain summoned all the crew on deck. A fiddler and several pipers commenced a service with a naval hymn. One line with particular significance was sung with great gusto: "Oh, Heavenly Father, hear our pleas for these souls who perished on your seas."

Then Charles spoke of the old man's achievements, and the crew listened incredulously. Throughout that service, the crew gazed with great affection upon the old man and his foundling. There was no shame in their death, and they remained restfully at peace.

Charles ordered them to beach the longboat at Sandy Cove and the fisherman and the merchild were stretched up to the mission. There, the old man was buried beside his wife and his foundling.

A Poor Fisherman's Rich Legacy

Many admirers paid homage. The fisherman's grave was lined with momentous gifts from all the orphans and lepers. Seemingly worthless articles, such as driftwood, shells, and the like, each told a heartfelt story. A piece of driftwood was inscribed with the name PETER, Maud's husband. It was surely a salient tribute to an old man who had lost his wife tending to his needs.

The significance of a large fish skeleton was often explained by a grave attendant: "That fish was caught by the old man for the foundlings at the mission. During a period of great famine, it sustained them for a month."

Tourists visiting the grave had little appreciation for the true significance of these keepsakes. "Imagine that," remarked a snooty man to his female companion. "Some wretch has thrown a fish on a grave."

"Quite true, dear. It is quite outrageous!" she complained, wiping her eye in a tearful manner with an embroidered handkerchief.

Over time, the greatest curiosity was a little wooden cart. It was said that a young man on crutches took up residence near the graves. He maintained them immaculately and ensured that none of the simple treasures from the poor was ever pilfered.

The spirit of the old man burns brightly to this day. And the residents still hold his kind, selfless ways closest to their hearts. Journey around the District of Tumby, and you will marvel at locations so aptly named by the old man: the Sentinel, Black Rock, and the ruins of Jacob's Ladder.

Sadly, in distant communities, where the old man's caring example was not evident, the land folk have grown increasingly hard hearted. Beauty, wealth, and power have become the yardsticks by which a meaningful life is measured.

And on the stormiest of nights, as the waves crash over the land bridge, one can imagine the old man lying in his bed under the apprehension that his wife's spirit is close at hand. "Nothing is as powerful as the wind," he respectfully told her, "And the sea is her servant."